BREVARD COUNTY LIBRARY SYSTEM
308 FORREST AVENUE
COCOA, FL 32922-7781

COCOA BEACH PUBLIC LIBRARY
55 S. Brevard Avenue
Cocoa Beach, Florida 32931

3 2480 00040 8449

COCOA BEACH LIBRARY

P9-BAV-451

First published in the United States 1992 by Chronicle Books. Copyright © 1991 by Tetsuya Honda. North American text based on the English translation made by Susan Matsui — copyright © 1992 by Chronicle Books. All rights reserved. First published in Japan by Fukutake Publishing Company, Tokyo under the title "Dosanko-Uma No Fuyu."

Printed in Singapore.
ISBN 0-8118-0251-1

Library of Congress Cataloging-in-Publication Data Available.

Distributed in Canada by Raincoast Books, 112 East Third Avenue, Vancouver, B.C., V5T 1C8

10 9 8 7 6 5 4 3 2

Chronicle Books
275 Fifth Street
San Francisco, California 94103

PROPERTY OF
BREVARD COUNTY LIBRARY SYSTEM

WILD HORSE WINTER

Tetsuya Honda

COCOA BEACH PUBLIC LIBRARY
55 S. Brevard Avenue
Cocoa Beach, Florida 32931

Chronicle Books ● San Francisco

One spring, a wild colt was born. All through the summer, he nibbled tender grasses. As the trees lost their leaves, he grew taller.

By the time the mountain peaks were
dusted with snow, the colt had grown
a thick coat to keep him warm during
the cold months yet to come.

The days grew shorter. Storm clouds darkened the winter sky, and each day was colder than the last. Then, the snow came to the colt's prairie, too.

Day after day, it fell—covering the land in a white stillness and burying the colt's favorite grasses under the deep drifts.

The horses chewed on bare branches and tore bark from the trees. The colt's mother searched for food, but there was none to be found.

Desperate, the horses left the prairie to search for food.

As the horses wandered through the forest, the snow began to fall more fiercely.

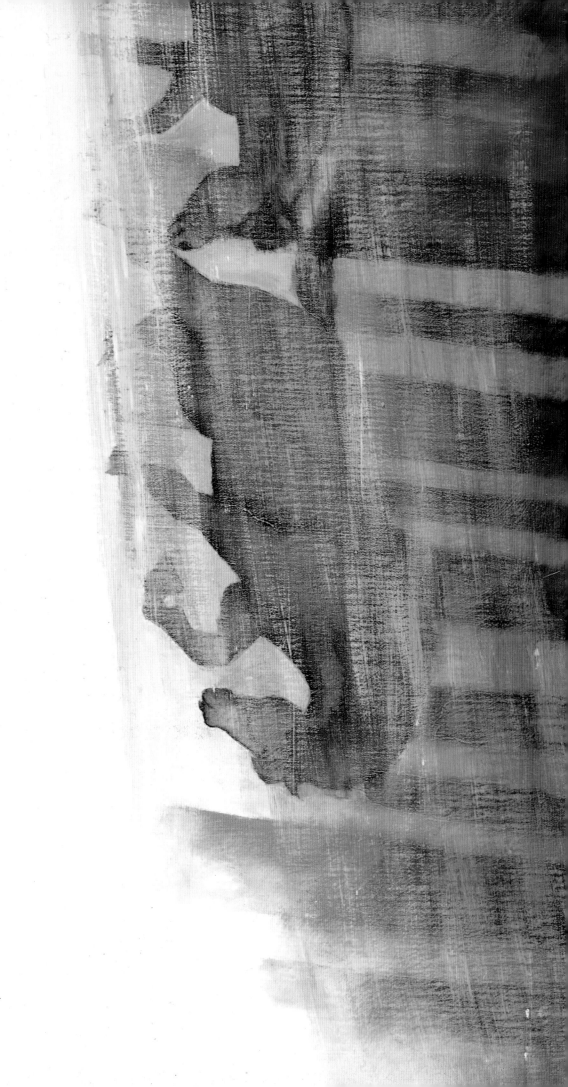

The wind was so strong that the colt could barely move. He followed in the footprints that his mother left in the deep snow.

The wind blew and blew, and the snowstorm became a raging blizzard. Cold and afraid, the colt huddled against his mother. She nuzzled him with her soft face to help keep him warm.

All around them, the drifts grew deeper.

The anxious colt struggled to keep his head above the snow.

It snowed until the drifts were so deep that the horses couldn't move. Soon they were almost completely buried. And, still the snow came swirling down from the sky.

Until, in the dark of the night, the blizzard finally passed and calm returned to the forest. The stars sparkled in the still night sky, and strange puffs of steam rose from the ground, but the horses were nowhere to be seen.

Slowly, the night turned into morning.

Suddenly, a horse burst through the drifts. He shook the snow from his mane and whinnied in the bright morning light. Then came another. The colt, too, eagerly dug his way out of the snow. His eyes searched the sunny forest for the other horses. The colt's mother was right beside him.

Once more, the horses continued their journey. At the edge of the forest they crossed a river.

The water was cold and the current was strong, but the colt swam close to his mother, and together they made it to the other side.

One by one, the horses followed the banks of the river through a great salt marsh, until, at last they arrived at the sea.

The colt had never seen the sea before. He stood with his mother and watched the waves roll across the sand. They had finally found what they were looking for.

The hungry horses began to eat kelp they found washed up along the shore. When the colt finished eating, he pranced in the waves and chased the squawking gulls.

After their feast, the horses galloped along the beach. The colt raced behind them.

He had survived his first winter. Soon it would be spring again, bringing new colts to the herd.